STORY
JUKKA LAAJARINNE

ILLUSTRATIONS
TIMO MÄNTTÄRI

SPY
DAD

Pikku Publishing

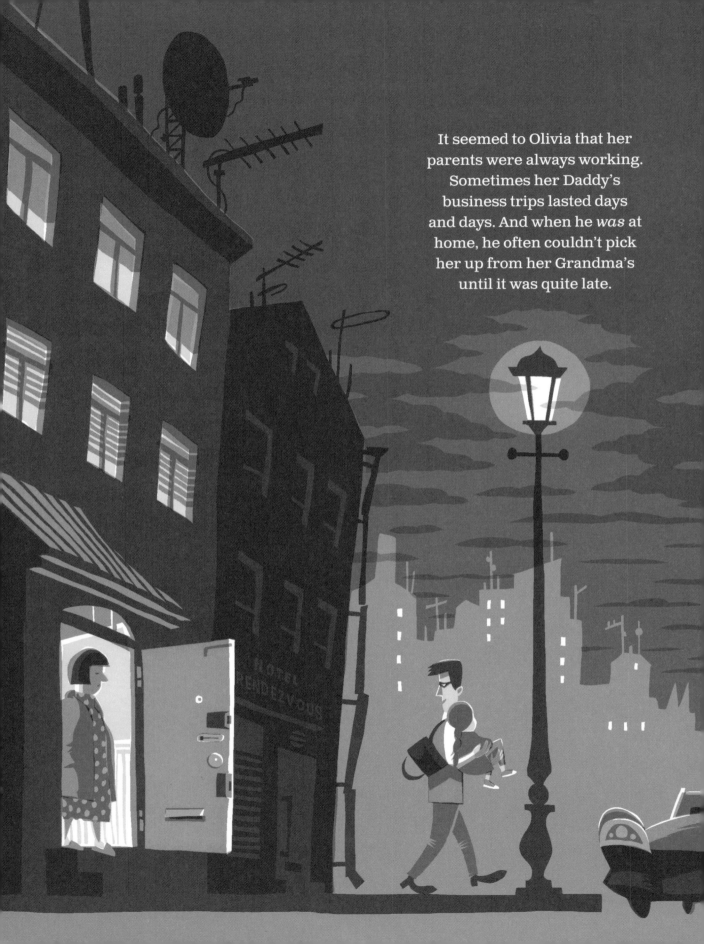

It seemed to Olivia that her parents were always working. Sometimes her Daddy's business trips lasted days and days. And when he *was* at home, he often couldn't pick her up from her Grandma's until it was quite late.

One evening, Olivia decided to speak her mind. 'I really wish you were at home more. Sophia's Mummy is at home every day...'

Darling Olivia, you know we...' began her mother.
'Actually, it's not *totally* out of the question,' interrupted her father.
'But...' her mother tried again, before her father announced, 'I'm going to stop work tomorrow – I'm going to resign!'

Morning came, and the doorbell rang. Olivia's father opened the door, and a visitor came into the kitchen.

'This is Agent Doubleday from my office,' said her father.
'We heard you are thinking of leaving?' said Agent Doubleday, looking rather serious.
'Could you possibly reconsider? You are very valuable to our work.'
But Olivia's father had made up his mind, and said so.

'Hello, you're Olivia, aren't you?' said Agent Doubleday. 'How's school going?' he asked gloomily, but before Olivia could answer, he had turned and gone.

There was a knock on the classroom door. It was Olivia's Daddy.
He had come to collect her early!

'Now that I've left my job, we've got all the time in the world.' said Olivia's father. 'How about a holiday right now?'
'Right now?'
'Yes, right now! I've talked to your teacher and it's all agreed.'

But it didn't all go as planned at the airport. When Daddy tried to buy the plane tickets, the attendant said, 'Your card doesn't appear to be working, sir.'

'What's going on, Daddy?' asked Olivia. Daddy thought for a moment, then explained, 'I think it means that if you don't go to work, your money may run out. But luckily, I've got money in my wallet. Boat tickets don't cost as much, so let's take a boat trip!'

But as they arrived at the port, Daddy seemed to have second thoughts. 'You know Olivia, these big ships are actually very noisy things, and we wouldn't get much peace.'

PASSPORTS AND I.D. WHILE YOU WAIT TEL: 857

'So I'm thinking
we should take a
road trip. Shall we
see how fast this
car can go?'

THE COVERT CAFÉ

'Daddy,' said Olivia, 'I'm getting hungry, and I need the toilet.'
So they stopped at a petrol station for something to eat.

But just as they were leaving, something happened to the car.

'Well, Olivia – what would you say to a hike?' said her father. 'We could wander through the woods. Goodbye to rushing everywhere!' he smiled, and threw his phone away. 'I really don't need this every minute of the day.'

'We'll eat our beans cold today,' said Daddy as they sat down for a picnic. 'We'd need to ask permission to light a fire, and that we can't do.' But the food tasted good in the fresh air of the woods.

Olivia and her Daddy slept under a fir tree that starry night. In the darkness, Daddy explained to Olivia how some people who don't work and are very poor always sleep outdoors.

The next morning, they knocked on the door of a farmhouse.
'Good morning,' said Olivia's father. 'May we please use your phone?
We'll be very quick.'

Olivia's father called home.

'So, here we are and...um...actually, I'm not sure where...yes, yes, everything's just fine...great actually...yes...*really*?...did they say that?' After a silence, he sighed and then smiled. 'OK, let's do that then. I think it's a good solution.'

'Olivia,' said Daddy. 'What do you think?
Have we had enough of holidaying? I'm afraid I may
need to earn some more money soon.'

'But I don't want it to finish...'
Olivia answered, disappointed. She didn't want to go back
to school just as the adventure was getting started.

'Yes, I know,' said her father.
'And I did use to spend far too much time away from home. But that's
going to change right now: they say I can do my job part-time.

Olivia wondered what that meant.

'It means that I won't stop working altogether. I'll just work less and have more time to spend with you!'

'You know, endless holidays aren't easy for me,' sighed Daddy.
'They aren't,' agreed the farmer. 'It's important to have something to do.'

'Please mister, what's your kitten's name?' Olivia asked.
'None of them have got names yet,' answered the farmer.
'Do you think it could be Tinker?' asked Olivia.
'I'm sure it could!' the farmer smiled.

'Look, Mummy! There's Daddy! Hey, Daddy! Down here!' cried Olivia.
'There he is! Hello up there!' cried her mother.
'Hello you down there! I'll pick you up from school Olivia!
Go straight to the entrance!
At 3 o'clock, OK?' cried her father.

Jukka Laajarinne is a Finnish author who has previously won the Nordic Picture Book Award (*Granny's Machine*, 2005), and received two nominations for the prestigious Finlandia Junior Prize (*Wiggly Figures*, 2003; *Spy Dad*, 2013). He enjoys success across several genres, writing not only children's books but also novels, science fiction, short stories and essays.

Timo Mänttäri is a Finnish illustrator and versatile graphic designer whose work includes children's books, book jackets, film graphics, postcards and posters. He lives and works in Helsinki, where he enjoys old films and bookshops, playing Lego with his two daughters and exploring the city on foot.

Other titles by Pikku Publishing

The Daisy and Daddy Story Books by Markus Majaluoma:

Let's Go to the Beach! • *Let's Read a Story!* • *Let's Have Lunch!* • *Let's Go on a Journey!*

This edition published in the United Kingdom in 2017 by
Pikku Publishing, 7 High Street, Barkway, Hertfordshire, SG8 8EA
www.pikkupublishing.com

ISBN: 978-0-9934884-5-0

Copyright in this edition © 2017 Pikku Publishing
© Jukka Laajarinne, Timo Mänttäri and WSOY
First published by Werner Söderström Ltd in 2013 with the Finnish title *Isä vaihtaa vapaalle*
Published by arrangement with Bonnier Rights Finland, Helsinki
Copyright in translation © Pikku Publishing
Translated by Anja Mannion

F I
L I

Pikku Publishing acknowledges the kind support of FILI in the production of this edition.

1 3 5 7 9 10 8 6 4 2

Printed in India by Replika Press Pvt. Ltd.